THE PALLIWOGGLES WERE HUGE AND SCARY!
GO TO SLEEP, NOW.
GO SLEEPY!
SWEET DREAMS!

IT'S A SUNNY
TEAC
STUDE
GOTT
HURR
COMING THROUGH!

AT GOODHEART ACADEMY.
S ARE TEACHING,
ARE STUDENTING.
NO TIME!
SORRY!
WATCH OUT!

IN THE CAFETORIUM...

THIS SCHOOL YEAR HAS BEEN OUT OF CONTROL!

I KNOW!
SAVING THE
GALAXY TWICE!

I MEANT HOMEWORK.

I HARDLY
EVER SEE
YOU
LATELY.

I'M GLAD WE'RE ALL TOGETHER
FOR A CHANGE.

POSEY
ULTRA-SPARKLE!

ANNA
ULTRA-BOOST!

LYRIC
ULTRA-SONIC!
GIRLS ROCK!

SKY
ULTRA-BRAINZ!

WHERE'S MORFRAN?
HE'S ALWAYS LATE.
HIS LOCKER'S ON THE DIAMETRICALLY OPPOSITE SIDE OF THE SCHOOL.
AM I TOO LATE TO GET MY OWN PAGE?
BTDT. WE ALL HAVE HAD OUR SCHOOL CHALLENGES. MINE WAS GETTING MY LOCKER OPEN. SO, LET'S GIVE MORFRAN A PAGE:
MORFRAN PITTS
FROM PLANET ROTERRA
INVENTOR!
BOOK OF M·E·A·N N·I·C·E

MORFRAN NEEDED A BOOST.
TBH, SCHOOL ISN'T GOING SO WELL FOR HIM.
WHAT IS THIS? A MODEL OF LOKIRA'S SUN?
HELLO! YOU'RE MISSING AT LEAST 43,952 ELEMENTS ON THIS TABLE!

CHECK OUT MY WRATH-BADGERS! ARENT THEY THE CRUELIST?!
DOOM & GLOOM

LUNCH IS OVER!

PICK UP YOUR TRASH!!!

BYE, MORFRAN.

SEE YOU IN STUDY HALL!
I THINK I'M GOING TO THE SCIENCE LAB.

LATER...
TALENT SHOW SIGN-UPS:
HEY MORFRAN!

HEY...

I THOUGHT YOU WEREN'T COMING.
SCIENCE LAB IS CLOSED-
IT SMELLS WEIRD?
EARLIER...
HEE-HEE...
COUGH!
COUGH!
COUGH!
COUGH!
COUGH!
EH-EHM. SO! I DON'T SEE YOU AS MUCH SINCE I MOVED IN WITH Z.
OH! MY PARENTS WANT YOU TO COME FOR DINNER SOMETIME.
BE THERE TONIGHT!

SWRP, SWRP, CRUNCH! MUNCH!
HOW'S SCHOOL, MORFRAN?
CHALLENGING.
MY TEACHER HAS DECLINED ALL OF MY SCIENCE PROJECT SUGGESTIONS.
SKY, DID YOU DECIDE ON YOURS?

IT'S ON THE 5 R'S!
Refuse
Reduce
Reuse
Repurpose
Recycle
I BETTER GO WORK ON IT.
BYE, MORFRAN!

AUGH! SO BORED!
I USED TO BE SO SPARKED!
I COULD FILL AN ENTIRE BOOK IN A NIGHT!
MOTHER, WHEN R U COMING FOR ME? I MISS MY WRATH BADGERS.
MOMMY:
Soon. Very soon.
GIVE SCRITCHES TO DOOM AND GLOOM!
MOMMY:
Don't forget to practice your piano. Good bye.
TALENT SHOW SIGN-UPS:
PIANO!
WOO-HOO!
BRAVO!
THAT'S IT!
I'LL PLAY EARTH-PIANO IN THE SCHOOL TALENT SHOW! MOMMY WILL DEFINITELY COME SEE ME PERFORM!

THE TALENT SHOW'S A GREAT IDEA, MORFRAN! A NORMAL THING!
I DIDN'T KNOW YOU PLAYED PIANO.

Z DOESN'T HAVE A PIANO. I CAN'T PRACTICE FOR THE SHOW.

YOU INVENT THINGS! MAKE ONE!
JUST PRACTICE IN THE MUSIC ROOM AT SCHOOL.
GO SIGN UP.

I WISH I COULD DO THE TALENT SHOW. BUT I'M SO BUSY.
SWOOSH!

I'M SO TIRED.

I'M SO OVERWHELMED!!!

ATTENTION, STUDENTS!
PLEASE WELCOME SUPERINTENDENT CONSTANCE TROLLA. SHE COMES FROM...
WAIT, WHERE?
NOT AROUND HERE. FAR... FAR AWAY.
ANOTHER SCHOOL DISTRICT, FAR FAR AWAY.

AND I SUPERINTEND
TO MAKE SOME CHANGES
AROUND HERE!

INTENSE.

I WONDER WHAT CHANGES?

OO! MAYBE SHE'LL REPLACE THE TEACHERS WITH LLAMAS!

SQUISH!

EW.
IS THAT GUM?

NO TALKING DURING LUNCH!
EVER!
I LIKE THIS.

DO YOU?

I'VE BEEN TRYING TO IMPLEMENT THAT FOR YEARS!
INTERESTING. MAYBE WE CAN BE ALLIES?
YOU WANT TO RULE THE CAFETORIUM. I WANT TO RULE THE UNIV... ERR SCHOOL!

HURRY UP, SQUAD!
SQUISH!
SQUISH!

EW!

HEY! YOU'RE TRACKING GUM ON MY BUS!
SQUISH!
SQUISH!
SQUISH!

SORRY!

IT WON'T COME OFF!
THAT'S WEIRD GUM.
IT LOOKS LIKE SNEEZE-GOO.

AT HOME...

HAHA!
HEHE!
HEHE!

EARTH DAY TRASH PICK UP? HMM...

PAPI IS WORKING LATE. I'M HERE.
I MISS MAMI.

I MISS MAMI, TOO.
TOCA UNA CANCIÓN.

¡SI!

$i^2 := -1; j^2 := -1; k^2 := -1$
$S(\alpha, T) = \frac{2}{\pi}\int_0^\pi \frac{\sin \alpha t}{t} dt$
$P(\eta_\infty < x) = F(x)$

MY LOCKER WON'T OPEN I HAVE A TEST TOMORROW POP QUIZ MY PEN EXPLODED ON MY FACE MY ART PROJECT DOESN'T LOOK GOOD I DIDN'T MAKE THE TEAM MY FRIEND IS MAD AT ME I
THE HALLWAY I WAS LATE TO GYM CLASS I FORGOT MY SCIENCE TEXTBOO

THE NEXT DAY...
SUP!
MORFRAN, HOW ARE THINGS AT Z'S?
GOOD! SHE MAKES A GREAT LASAGNA AND HELPED ME FOR MY HISTORY QUIZ. THO EARTH IS ONLY 4.5 BILLION YEARS OLD, SO THERE'S NOT THAT MUCH TO KNOW.

I COULDN'T SLEEP LAST NIGHT!
I HAD SCARY DREAMS.
REMEMBER WHAT JANE SAID: IF YOU DREAM IT, YOU CAN DO IT!

I THINK THAT'S THE OPPOSITE OF WHAT YOU WANT FOR NIGHTMARES.
I MISS THE PALLIES!

I MISS THE PALLIES!
I SENSE A DISTRESS CALL!
THE SQUAD NEEDS US!
?
I SMELL THAT!

TAP!
PALLIES!
WE MISS YOU!

HI! FROM I, THE GREAT MORFRAN.
YOU'RE STILL THERE? BEHAVING?

HE IS, BOB.
LITERALLY JUST TALKING ABOUT YOU!

WE HEARD YOUR DISTRESS CALL!

WE ARE STRESSED!
THIS WILL BE A DE-STRESS CALL!
WHAT'S GOING ON?

THANKS FOR BEING THERE FOR US.
TAKE A BREAK! GO HAVE SOME FUN!!
A GREAT WAY TO HELP YOU DE-STRESS IS TO TALK TO A TRUSTED PAL.

OVER AND OUT!

HAVING FUN TOGETHER DOES SOUND... WELL, FUN!
YAY! LET'S DO IT!

Z SAID SHE'D TAKE ME TO SOMETHING CALLED A "MAWL" IF YOU WISH TO COME!

YES!

YOLO!
THE SQUAD IS GETTING A MUCH DESERVED BREAK AND HAVING SOME FUN!

?
??

IS THIS KETCHUP?
IS THIS PESTO?
NEW RECIPE!
YUCK!

ATTENTION!
ATTENTION PLEASE!
I HAVE DECIDED TO BREAK UP THE SCHOOL - FOR GOOD.
WUT?!

FOUR NEW SCHOOL DISTRICTS!
FOUR DIFFERENT SCHOOLS!
HUH?
WHAT?
GASP

OH NO!
THIS IS HORRIBLE!
WE'RE GOING TO BE SEPARATED.
WHERE'S Z'S HOUSE?
ON A DIFFERENT DIMENSION.
I WONDER WHICH SCHOOL DISTRICT.

YES, YOU'LL ALL BE SPLIT UP!
GOODBYE, GOODHEART!

WE SHOULD GO SEE Z. FIND OUT WHAT'S GOING ON.

I NEED EXTRA TIME TO GET TO MY LOCKER.
GO AHEAD.

WHERE'S Z?
SHE IS ON A MUCH-NEEDED VACATION.
SHE DESERVES A LITTLE BREAK, DOESN'T SHE?

I NEED YOUR HELP. FOLLOW ME.
EXCEPT SKY, YOU STAY HERE AND COVER MY DESK.

TAKE THOSE SIGNS DOWN!
BE YOURSELF!
STAY
POSIT

NOPE.
THAT'S NOT RIGHT.
FLIP!
NOPE!
FLIP!
THAT'S NOT IT.

ARE YOU LOOKING FOR SOMETHING?

I THINK YOU MAY KNOW WHAT I'M LOOKING FOR.

I DO?

A SPECIAL SIGN. A *VERY SPECIAL* SIGN.

OH! I DO KNOW!

I KNEW IT!
You are very special!

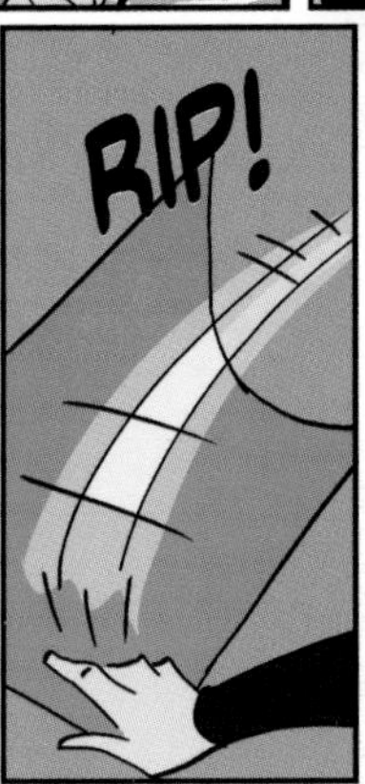
RIP!

FLIP!
THAT'S ALL YOU GOT?
FLIP!
YOU ARE VERY SPECIAL!
AN IMPORTANT MESSAGE, I AGREE.

UH, DOES ANYONE KNOW WHERE Z IS?
SHE'S NOT IN HER OFFICE?

THE SUPERINTENDENT SAID SHE'S AWAY? YOU DIDN'T KNOW?

IS SKY AROUND?

UH, I THINK SHE'S STAYING LATE IN THE LAB.

OH FINE.

COME OVER TO MY HOUSE.

I MISS Y
MAMI.

SHE'S FAR
AWAY.

SO IS
MINE.

YOUR MOM'S
PROTECTING
YOUR
COUNTRY.

SHE'S A
HERO.

YOU'RE
PRETTY
MUCH A
HERO!

So weird today
Where is Z?
SUPERINTENDENT WANTS TO SPLIT UP THE SCHOOLS. 😢💔

AND HAS A WEIRD DISLIKE FOR POSTERS?
DO YOU THINK ROCKS HAVE DREAMS?

YES, THE DRESS REHEARSAL, WHERE YOU RUN THROUGH A SHOW AS IF IT WERE THE REAL THING! I'M SURE IT WILL GO SMOOTHLY.
TOOT!
TOOT!
TOOT!
ARE YOU NERVOUS, MORFRAN?
NOPE!
EXCITED TO SHOW MOMMY MY MASTERPIECE.
!!!
HUH?
WHAT IS THAT?

WHAT EVEN IS THAT THING?
THAT KID IS *NOT* NORMAL.

HA! HA!

DON'T BE BOTHERED! JUST PLAY!

HA! HA!
PLAY IT!

THERE'S NO WAY I CAN GO OUT THERE AGAIN.

I'LL NEVER FIT IN HERE...

HUH?

Z?!
MWAHAHAHA!
THIS IS THE DIABOLICAL PLAN TO FINALLY RULE THE CAFETERIA!

MEANWHILE, ON PALIDORIA...

I SMELL TROUBLE!

TO THE SHIP!

THE GIRLS NEED OUR HELP!

LET'S GO!
ZOOM!

GO AHEAD!
BLAST!!!
TRY TO ESCAPE!
SLIME·A·TRON
SPLAT!!!

SPLAT!
SPLAT!
BLAST!
SQUISH!

WE HAVE TO SAVE Z!
Z! WE'RE COMING FOR YOU!

SPLAT!
SQUISH!
WHOA!
SLIDE!

Z! WE'RE NOT COMING FOR YOU!

ANNA!
USE YOUR ULTRA-BOOST!

HA, HA, HA!
BLAST!
CAN WE USE OUR POWERS?
WE'RE SUPPOSED TO BE ULTRA-SECRET AND CLASSIFIED.
PAGE 3 IN THE GUIDE-BOOK.
ULTRA SQUAD
CONFIDENTIAL
SKY
ANNA

MUAHAHAHAHAHA!!!!!
AREN'T YOU TERRIFIED?

HA! HA!
IT'S JUST SLIME!
NICE!

SLIME IS DE-STRESSING! HA, HA!

WAIT! YOU'RE NOT SUPPOSED TO HAVE FUN!
YOU'RE SUPPOSED TO BE TRAPPED AND TERRIFIED!
SLIME-A-

WASN'T A VERY GOOD PLAN.

GRRR!

EVERYONE IS DISTRACTED.
PERFECT!
NOBODY'S WATCHING! WE CAN UNLEASH OUR ULTRA-POWERS.

THEY DON'T WORK--
OH DEAR. POSEY'S ULTRA-ARM...

LYRIC'S ULTRA-GUITAR...

ANNA'S ULTRA-LEGS ALL STUCK IN SLIME!
BUT ...WHAT A MINUTE.

SKY...?
YOUR BRAINS AREN'T STUCK...

KKK Z Z KRRR Z Z Z THKK Z Z!!!
HUH?
WHAT'S THAT SOUND?

ZKKRKKK!!
AAAA AARGHH H H!!!!
SLAM!
SPLASH!
SLAM!
UMMPHHH!!
SQUISH!

AAAAAARRGH!!

WHAT IS THAT?!
DON'T KNOW!
EVEN MY ULTRABRAINZ ARE STUMPED!

AARRGHHHHHHH!!
WHAT'S MY WORMHOLIA BACK-IN-TIME MACHINE DOING HERE?

LOOK!

ZZZZZZZ

KRRRR

SUPERINTENDENT!
SUPERINTENDENT!

LOOK, I'M RULING THE LUNCH ROOM!

ARE YOU, YOURSELF, STUCK IN THE SLIME?

ER...
WELL, I SEE YOU'VE TRAPPED MY NEMESIS, I'LL GIVE YOU THAT CREDIT.
HELLO, Z!

LOOKS LIKE YOU'RE HAVING AN EXTENDED LUNCH BREAK.
MUAHAH!

YOU WON'T GET AWAY WITH THIS!

GET AWAY WITH WHAT, EXACTLY?

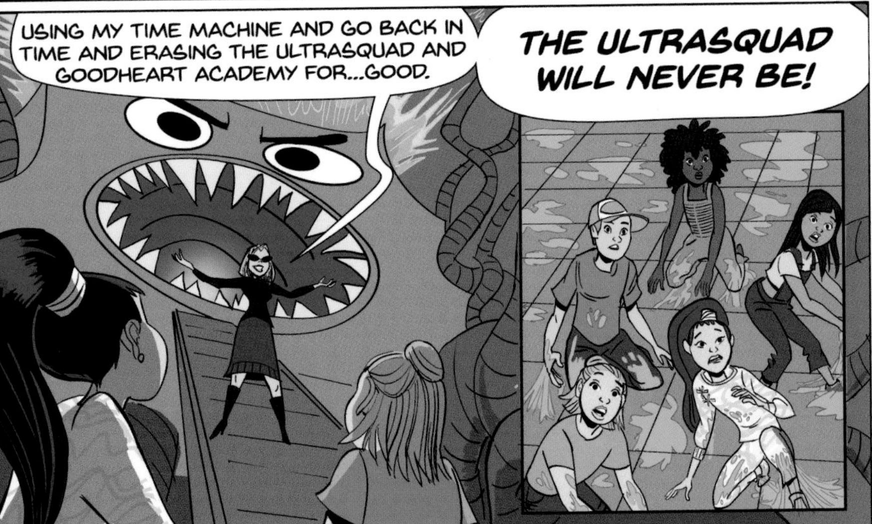
USING MY TIME MACHINE AND GO BACK IN TIME AND ERASING THE ULTRASQUAD AND GOODHEART ACADEMY FOR...GOOD.
THE ULTRASQUAD WILL NEVER BE!

AND THEN, I CAN RULE THE WORLD!

BUT HOW DID YOU, THE SUPERINTENDENT, GET MY WORMHOLIA TIME MACHINE PROTOTYPE?

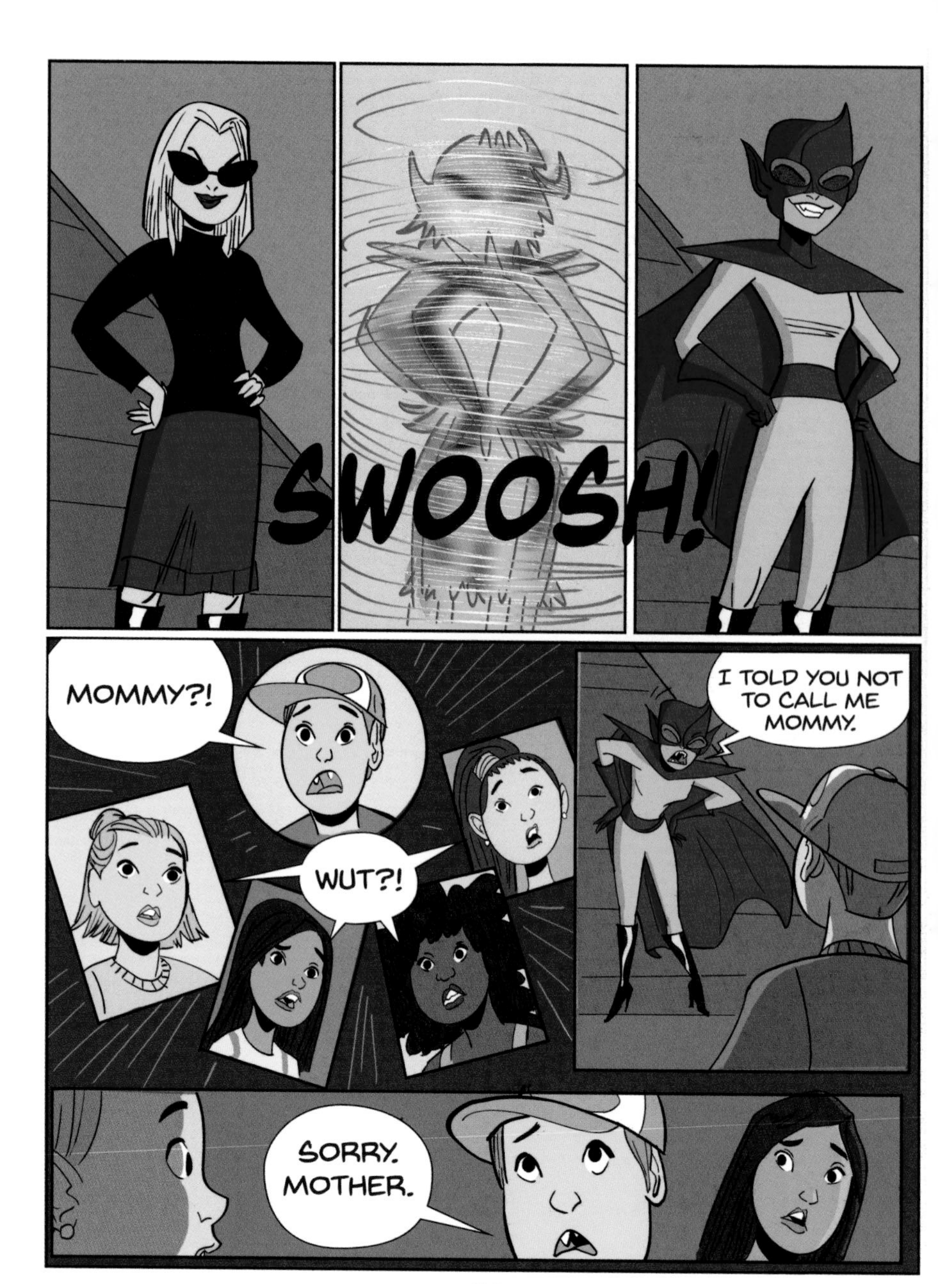
SWOOSH!
MOMMY?!
WUT?!
I TOLD YOU NOT TO CALL ME MOMMY.
SORRY. MOTHER.

I'M GOING TO PRESS THAT SWITCH AND --

IT'S JUST A PROTOTYPE. IT NEVER EVER WORKED.

OH BUT FRANNY, IT DOES.

FLASHBACK TO BOOK 3!
PALIRIDIUM! THE STRONGEST METAL IN THE KNOWN UNIVERSE.
I BET THAT WOULD WORK REALLY WELL FOR MY...
ALL IT TOOK WAS A LITTLE MATERIAL FROM PALIDORIA...

AND YOU LED ME RIGHT TO IT!

SLAP!!!

NOW, THE VORTEXX WILL WIN!
AND U.L.T.R.A WILL LOSE!

WINNER!

LOSER!

GOOD THING I CHOSE WISELY WHEN I NEEDED A SIDEKICK.

ISN'T THAT RIGHT...
FRANNY?

I FOUND HIM AT AN ORPHANAGE ON ROTERRA - ASSEMBLING HIS PACIFIER RELOADING MACHINE FOR THE OTHER CHILDREN.

THAT'S WHEN I KNEW...

HE WAS THE ONE.

SO I TOOK HIM.
WUT?!?
WAIT,
WUT?!

THEN I RAISED HIM, ALONE AND LONELY...
TO INVENT THINGS FOR ME.

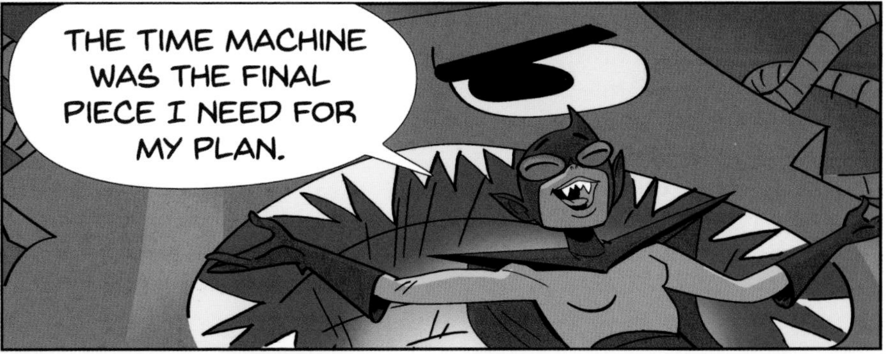
THE TIME MACHINE WAS THE FINAL PIECE I NEED FOR MY PLAN.

!!!...
OH NO! IF SHE GOES BACK IN TIME AND REVERSES THE UNIVERSAL LEGEND, EVERYTHING THAT HAPPENED IN BOOKS 1-3 WILL BE ERASED!

ULTRA SQUAD
THE GIRLS WOULDN'T HAVE JOINED THE ULTRASQUAD!
OR MET Z OR THE PALLIES!
RECRUITMENT OFFICER FOR THE...
ULTRA-CLASSIFIED
ULTRA-INTER-GALACTIC
AGENCY OF
ULTRA!
I WAS SO NOT EXPECTING THAT.
PLEASURE TO MEET YOU.
COME TO THOSE WHO WAIT!
IT TOOK FIVE-EVER!
OR HAD ACCIDENTALLY GONE TO ALTER-EARTH!
THAT'S A STRANGE-LOOKING RAINBOW.
A STRANGEBOW!
BLAST!!
SWOSH!
AAAAAAAGH!
SPARKLES!
TO DEFEAT THE EVIL STRANGEBOW!
WOOT!
OR SAVE THE ALTER-SQUAD!
THEY WOULDN'T HAVE TRAVELED TO PALIDORIA!

THEY WOULDN'T HAVE MET THEIR ALTER-SELVES!

OR SAVED THE UNIVERSE!

TO SAVE THE GALAXY GLAM JAM!

NOW ALL I HAVE TO DO IS PRESS THAT SWITCH AND GO BACK IN TIME TO CHANGE THE LEGEND OF U.L.T.R.A!

MORFRAN, MAYBE YOU CAN HELP ME OUT AGAIN.
I NEED THE UNIVERSAL LEGEND.
I'VE TRACED IT TO GOODHEART ACADEMY! IT'S HERE SOMEWHERE.
WITH THE ULTRASQUAD.

UNIVERSAL LEGEND TELLS OF 4 HUMANS CHOSEN FOR THEIR
* CELESTIAL CREATIVITY *
* SUPERNOVA STRENGTH *
* COSMIC KINDNESS *
* ORBIT ORIGINALITY *
AND SOME WEIRDNESS, TOO!
SO THAT'S WHAT SHE'S BEEN LOOKING FOR.

WHY DO YOU NEED TO FIND IT NOW? CAN'T YOU JUST GO BACK IN TIME AND FIND IT?

OF COURSE I COULD! I JUST NEED TO KNOW... ER..UH...

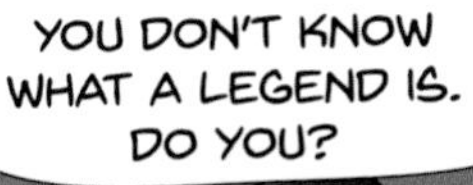
YOU DON'T KNOW WHAT A LEGEND IS. DO YOU?

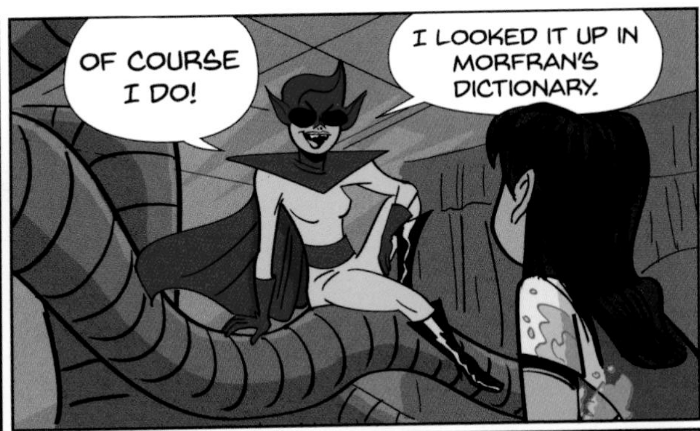
OF COURSE I DO!
I LOOKED IT UP IN MORFRAN'S DICTIONARY.

DEFINITION: LEGEND.
1. SOMEONE FAMOUS OR ADMIRED.

I TRIED THIS ROUTE AND CAME UP WITH NOTHING.

2. A VERY OLD STORY FROM ANCIENT TIMES.

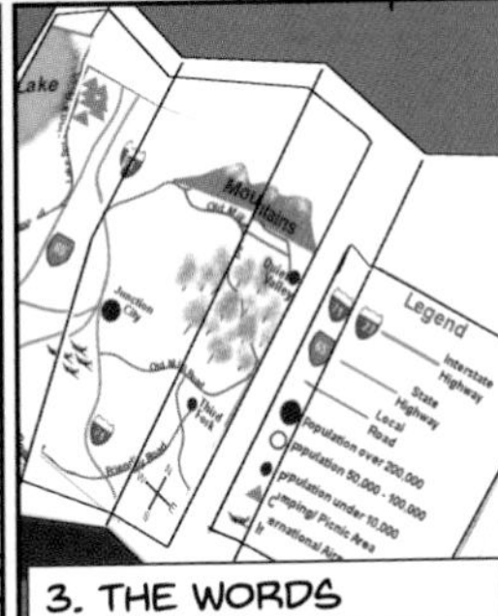
Lake
Legend
Interstate Highway
State Highway
Local Road
3. THE WORDS WRITTEN ON OR NEXT TO A PICTURE OR MAP THAT EXPLAIN WHAT IT IS ABOUT OR WHAT THE SYMBOLS ON IT MEAN.

I, IN MY INFINITE WISDOM, KNOW THAT IT'S #3!
SO I AM LOOKING FOR A MAP WITH SYMBOLS TO UNLOCK THE LEGEND!

ISN'T IT THE SECOND ONE?
SHH!

ZENOBIA, WE'VE WASTED ENOUGH TIME.
YOU KNOW IT'S MY DESTINY.
JUST TELL ME.
NO!

WE'VE KNOWN EACH OTHER A LONG TIME.

YOU HAVE?!!

WE WERE NEVER FRIENDS.
HA! REMEMBER IN FIFTH GRADE I MADE THAT BOOK OF M.E.A.N. AND PASSED IT AROUND SO EVERYONE COULD READ IT? HAHAHA!
HA!
OH, I REMEMBER.
YOU WROTE THAT I WAS A "SCALEY NERD."

REMEMBER WHEN I GAVE YOU YOUR FIRST BOOK OF MEAN, MORFRAN?

I USED IT FOR INVENTIONS! NOT FOR WORLD DOMINAT...

...OH WAIT.

??

OK, MAYBE MY INVENTIONS WERE TO CONTROL WITH THE UNIVERSE. BUT I DIDN'T KNOW ANY BETTER!

AND NOW YOU KNOW WHY! I'VE RAISED YOU TO BE ...
MEAN!

GOODHEART ACADEM
I'VE CHANGED. I GO TO GOODHEART ACADEMY NOW!
WE STAND FOR KINDNESS HERE!

WAIT...

EART ACADEMY
WHY IS THAT ASKEW?

WOOSH!

GRAB!

PULL!

HA!

WOOHOO!
THIS IS IT!

BLA BLA...
4 HUMANS CHOSEN FOR
BLA BLA...
WHEN THE UNIVERSE IS
IN DANGER BLA BLA...
TOGETHER AS A SECRET.
I CAME ALL THE WAY
HERE, THROUGH SPACE
AND TIME...
Offer valid only on participating planets. Not to be combined with other offers real or implied. Limited to four earthlings per millennia. Please present this scroll to the chosen ones on a sunny school day. This option must be exercised before the end of the second grading period ending at the expiry of 2200 years of the last survivor of all lineal descendants of the late Ethereal Constantinople Urilius. Eh, nobody reads these anyway.

AND NOW I AM READY
TO ERASE YOU-

IS THAT AN ERASER...?
VERY
LITERAL.

I AM GOING BACK TO THE
MOMENT WHEN THE SCROLL
WAS WRITTEN AND ADD
MY NAME!
ONE OF YOU WILL BE
REPLACED-

WHAT'S YOUR
NAME?
STELLA.

I'LL ERASE STELLA AND PUT... MY NAME!
HM...STELLA.... I DON'T SEE THE NAME STELLA, YET... ALL I NEED IS TO ERASE IT AND PUT IN MINE AND THEN I WILL BE A MEMBER OF THE ULTRASQUAD!
YOU WANT TO BE A MEMBER OF THE ULTRASQUAD?
YES!
I WANT ALL THE POWERS! PLUS, IT'S BORING TO BE WORKING ALONE.
I WILL LEAD AND YOU THREE WILL FOLLOW.

WHAT ABOUT ME?

YOU DID YOUR JOB.
THE TIME MACHINE WORKS.
YOU'RE NOW EXPENDABLE.
BUH-BYE.

WOA. SHE IS MEAN.
LEGIT TERRIBLE.
YUP!

ENOUGH BANTER!

I'VE WAITED LONG ENOUGH.
WHISTLE!

PLEASE NOTE WE REMAIN UNDERCOVER.
EARTHLINGS WILL NOT NOTICE US!

WE ARE NOT SPACE ALIENS!
I AM A SHEEP.
I COUNT SHEEP.
SLEEPY SHEEP!
I'M A MOUSE, DUH!
I A BURRITO!
PALLIES!!!

POSEY! I PICKED OUT MY OWN COSTUME FOR ONCE.
A FIRE-BREATHING FEROCIOUS BEING!
SO, YOUR EARTH-MATES WILL NOT THINK ANYTHING IS OUT OF THE ORDINARY!
THERE IS A HUGE ROBOT MONSTER, THE SUPERINTENDENT IS MORFRAN'S MOTHER WHO TURNS INTO A TORNADO, AND WE BEGAN THE EVENING WITH MORFRAN'S PIANO.
I THINK THE JIG IS UP.
??
CHOCO MILK
SNATCH!
CHOCO MILK YUM!
SPLASH!
GLURG!
GLURG!
GLURG!

WHOA!
THE CHOCOLATE MILK DISSOVLES THE SLIME!
NICE JOB, LOUIE!

HUGS!
KISSES!
SMOOCH!

MORFRAN.
BOB.

SO HAPPY TO SEE YOU!

TIME TO SAVE THE GALAXY!

MUAHAHAHAHAHAHA!!!
MY ROBOT ARMY!
MY ROBOT ARMY, NOW.

WE'RE OUT-NUMBERED.
ACTUALLY, WE'RE NOT.
GOODHEART ACADEMY!
WE NEED YOUR HELP!
WE STAND FOR...
BRAVERY! TEAMWORK! AND JUSTICE!

HUH?
WHAT'S GOING ON HERE?

SPLAT!

THOSE ARE BADDIES!
GET 'EM!

FOOD FIGHT!
SPLAT!
SPLAT!
WHAM!
SPLASH!

SPLAT!
??
WOOSH!!!
LET'S GO SAVE Z!

OOHH!
SPLASH!
SQUISH!
SPLASH!
RAVIOLI!
NOM!
NOM!
NOM!
RIP!!!
WOOSHH!
SNATCH!

HEY!
GIVE ME THAT!

WHERE DO YOU THINK YOU'RE GOING?

SPLASH!

GRRRR!

SPLAT!
SPLAT!
MY DUDES!
SPLASH!

IT ME!

AW! K, LET ME THROUGH.
I NEED YOUR HELP...

YOU DON'T HAVE TO DO THIS, MOMMY. YOU COULD BE STAY HERE AND BE SUPERINTENDENT. WE COULD BE HAPPY HERE.
PFFT. HAPPY SHMAPPY.

AND DON'T CALL ME MOMMY.

CALL ME THE RULER OF THE GALAX--

UMPH!

SLAM!
CHOMP!

AAAAA
KKKKZZKK
DID YOU JUST...
...HURT HER? NO! OF COURSE NOT.
I SENT HER TO A PLACE WHERE MAYBE SHE CAN LEARN TO BE HAPPY. AND NICE TO OTHER PEOPLE.
YES, THAT LAND OF HAPPY STICK FIGURES. BOMBARDING US WITH LOVE.
WELCOME TO TUDEE... A HAPPY PLACE TUBEE...
HAPPY, HAPPY HAPPY HAPPY... TUMEE!
EVERYONE AROUND HERE IS *TUHAPPY*!
STOP! STOP STOP!!

OH COOL!
SHE ALSO GOT THE TRANSPORTAL TO WORK!

ZAP!!

SCREECH!
SCREECH!
SCREECH!
SCREECH!

DOOM!
GLOOM!

HEH...
OKAY...
THAT'S NICE?
GRRR
GRR
GRR

I NEED TO DEBRIEF THE AGENCY OF U.L.T.R.A.
WHY DON'T I TAKE THE WRATH BADGERS BACK TO THE HOUSE WITH ME?

ARE YOU SUPERHEROES?
WAS THAT A MONSTER?
WAS THE SCHOOL SECRETARY A GIANT LIZARD PERSON?

I DIDN'T KNOW DRAGONS ARE REAL?
WUT JUST HAPPENED?

IT'S ALMOST SHOWTIME KIDS!

HOW DID THE DRESS REHEARSAL GO?
HUH?

WHAT HAPPENED HERE?
IT WAS UH... SKIT! A SKIT FOR THE TALENT SHOW!

GREAT ACTING, WASN'T IT?

WOW, I ALMOST BELIEVED IT WAS REAL!
WOW! I THOUGHT IT WAS REAL.

MIGHT BE TOO HARD TO REPEAT. PROBABLY SHOULD GO ON WITH THE PLANNED SHOW.

CALL TIME IN 5!
LET'S GET RID OF THE EVIDENCE. I MEAN, THE PROPS.

WATCH OUT!
COMING THROUGH!!!

SWEEP!
DUST!
MOP!

SPARKLE!
SHINE!
SQUEAK!!

YOU READY TO PLAY, MORFRAN?
UH...

IT'S FOR THE BEST.
I'M NOT GOING UP THERE.
IT WAS A LOT.

WHAT IF WE BANDED TOGETHER TO SUPPORT YOU?
DID YOU SAY BAND?!
THAT'S MY JAM!
I'M READY FOR MY CLOSEUP!

I SING, LYRIC ON GUITAR.
SKY, DO YOU PLAY AN INSTRUMENT?
USING MY ULTRA-BRAINZ...

I CAN LEARN THE BASS IN...

...3 SECONDS!

OOH, OOH, MAY I PLAY DRUMS?
REMEMBER A BAD DRESS REHEARSAL MEANS A GREAT OPENING!!! THE SHOW MUST GO ON!

BUT MY PIANO --

CLANG!
CLING!
SLAM!
BAM!

GOOD TO GO!

THANKS, BOB, I KNOW YOU AND I HAVE HAD OUR DIFFERENCES.
MEH. YOU HAVEN'T NOT BEEN HELPFUL.

YOU NEVER DID GET TO DANCE AT THE GLAM-JAM.
HOW ABOUT THE ULTRASQUAD BAND WITH PALLIES BACKUP DANCERS?

DID SOMEONE SAY BACKUP DANCERS?
SHOWTIME!!!
TAP!
TAP!
TAP!
TAP!
EEP!
IT'S TIME!
I'M SO NERVOUS FOR THEM.

BREAK A LEG!

INTRODUCING...
THE ULTRASQUAD BAND!

HUH?

MAMI!!!
I'M SO PROUD OF YOU!
WE'RE PROUD OF YOU!
YOU'RE BOTH HEROES!

I'M SO HAPPY FOR YOUR BROTHER! AND YOU!

THAT'S REALLY NICE. I'M SORRY ABOUT YOUR MOTHER.
I FEEL TERRIBLE ABOUT HOW THAT WENT.

SHE WAS NEVER VERY KIND. OR SUPPORTIVE. SHE JUST MADE ME WORK FOR HER.

IT WOULD BE NICE TO HAVE A PARENT WHO...

N.I.C.E

Z!!!
SPOILER ALERT!
JUST SO WE DON'T WORRY TOO MUCH ABOUT POOR MORFRAN, LET'S FLASH FORWARD LIKE WE HAD A TIME MACHINE OR SOMETHING:

1 YEAR LATER:
THEY'RE SO PAILIDORABLE!
THAT TOOK FIVE-EVER!
GOOD THINGS COME TO THOSE WHO WAIT!

NOW:
GREAT WORK, ULTRASQUAD. INCLUDING MORFRAN.

AM I INCLUDED IN THE ULTRA-SQUAD?

YES!!!

THE ULTRASQUAD IS NOT EXCLUSIONARY. THANKS TO POSEY, ANNA, LYRIC, AND SKY FOR BEING OUR SQUAD TO TAKE DOWN THE VORTEXX. ULTRASQUAD IS ABOUT HAVING A GOOD HEART!
WELCOME TO THE ULTRASQUAD.

WHAT'S MY POWER?
ULTRA-HEART!

EVERYONE HELPED SAVE THE DAY, TODAY! WELCOME TO THE ULTRASQUAD.
CO
HARDWORKING!
YOUR ULTRA-POWER IS...
COUR

ENCE!
HELPFUL
LOYALTY!
POSITIVITY!
STRENGTH!
E!
INDEPENDENCE!
CREATIVITY!
KINDNESS!
ORIGINALITY!

X
AND YOU!

THE CREATORS

Author
Julia DeVillers is the author of books including TRADING FACES and THE AUDITION with Maddie Ziegler. Her book became the Disney Channel Original Movie READ IT AND WEEP.

Co-Author
R.R. Wells is a writer, producer, and director of animated short films. He is the co-author, with Julia DeVillers, of ULTRASQUAD and ULTRASQUAD: UNDER THE STRANGEBOW.

Illustrator
Rafael Rosado is the illustrator and co-creator of the graphic novel series GIANTS BEWARE, MONSTERS BEWARE, and DRAGONS BEWARE. He is currently a storyboard artist for Warner Brothers, Disney, and Cartoon Network.

Assistant Writer: Kylie Lovsey
Inker/Penciler: Dan Root
Colorist: John Novak
Production Manager: Kylie Lovsey
Letterer: Kylie Lovsey
Cover Designer: Kylie Lovsey
Assistant Visual Designer: Jay Graham
Assistant Visual Designer: Amy Marado
Assistant Visual Designer: Josh Jackson
Assistant Visual Designer: Brennan Kurfees
3D Artist: Patrick Danber
Producer: Jeremy Hughes

Special thanks to Kendra Stokes and Traci Graziani!

CRAVING MORE ULTRA-ADVENTURES?!

CHECK OUT OUR OTHER TITLES BELOW!

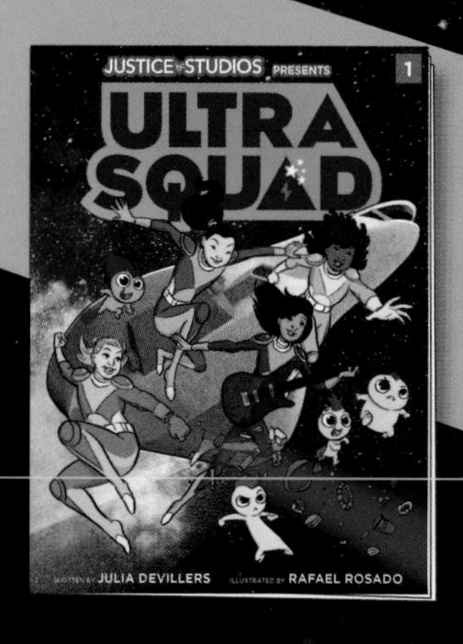

**

For information regarding the CPSIA on this printed material, call: (203) 595-3636 and provide reference #RICH - 826015.

Printed in the United States of America.

First edition.

ISBN-978-1-7327030-3-2